EATING UP GLADYS

By **MARGOT ZEMACH**
Illustrated by **KAETHE ZEMACH**

 ARTHUR A. LEVINE BOOKS
AN IMPRINT OF SCHOLASTIC INC.

Library of Congress Cataloging-in-Publication Data

Zemach, Margot.

Eating up Gladys / by Margot Zemach ;

illustrated by Kaethe Zemach.— 1st ed.   p. cm.

Summary: When Hilda and Rose get fed up with their older sister's bossiness,

they get revenge by threatening to have her for dinner.

ISBN 0-439-66490-X — ISBN 0-439-66491-8 (alk. paper)

[1. Sisters — Fiction. 2. Bossiness — Fiction.]

I. Zemach, Kaethe, ill. II. Title.   PZ7.Z416Eat 2005

[E]—dc22   2004023417

10 9 8 7 6 5 4 3 2 1   05 06 07 08 09

Book design by Elizabeth B. Parisi

First edition, October 2005

Printed in Singapore 46

To sisters everywhere

Gladys was the oldest sister.

Because she was older than Hilda and Rose,
Gladys was the first to be visited by the tooth fairy,
and the first to ride a two-wheel bike.

Because she was older than Hilda and Rose,
Gladys had a room of her own and stayed up late at night,
laughing and being important.

When their parents were out, Gladys was the one in charge.
Gladys was the only one allowed to take care of the baby,
or heat up food for their dinner.

Sometimes she was nice to her sisters;
but when Gladys was in charge, she was bossy.
When Gladys yelled, she could be heard a block away,
and when she stomped her foot, Hilda and Rose
usually did what she wanted.

One evening, when their parents were out,

Gladys was bossier than ever.

"Hilda and Rose!" Gladys commanded,

"Put away your toys, and set the table.

Then hang up your coats, and put your pajamas on.

And don't make any noise, because the baby is sleeping!"

But Hilda was tired of Gladys bossing her around.
"Gladys," said Hilda, "you are not the boss of me!"

"Oh, yes I AM the boss of you," snapped Gladys.
"I'm the one in charge! So put away your toys, set the table,
hang up your coats, and get your pajamas on. Now!
And don't forget; the baby's sleeping!"
Then Gladys stomped upstairs to her room.

"That's the end!" declared Hilda.
"Let's get rid of that bossy girl!
Let's have her for dinner,
and be done with her forever!"
Hilda and Rose rolled around laughing.
"Eating up Gladys! Ha, ha, ha!"

"Gladys is so big, we'll need a lot of dishes," said Hilda.

"That's for sure," said Rose. "A lot of dishes."

"And Gladys is so mean, she might not taste good," said Hilda.

"That's for sure," said Rose.

"We'll need good things to eat her with."

Hilda and Rose set the table for a feast.

"How will we cook that bossy girl?" Rose asked.

"In a pot," said Hilda. "In a really big pot."

"That's for sure," said Rose.

Hilda and Rose found the biggest pot
in the house, and marched upstairs
to get Gladys.

"Get ready, Gladys!" Hilda and Rose yelled
as they burst into Gladys's room.
"Your time is up! Your time is through!
We're having you for dinner!"

"Ha, ha, ha. Very funny," said Gladys.
"For your information, we're having
spaghetti for dinner tonight.
Go away and leave me alone.
Can't you see I'm busy?"

Hilda and Rose went back downstairs.

"I don't think she wants us to have her for dinner," said Rose.

"Well, too bad," said Hilda. "Too bad for her.

We're having her for dinner no matter what, and that's that."

Hilda and Rose made up a song
and sang it louder and louder:
"We'll eat her with spaghetti, and pickles and tomatoes!
We'll eat her up with jelly, and pudding and potatoes!
Eating up Gladys! Eating up Gladys! Eating up Gladys, NOW!"

"What on earth is going on?" Gladys hollered
as she ran downstairs and saw the mess in the kitchen.
"You're just in time, Gladys!" Hilda yelled.
"Get in the pot! Get in the pot!"

"Me?" roared Gladys. "Get in a pot? Never!"
"Oh, come on, Gladys. Just *try* it!" begged Rose.

"Are you crazy or something?"
Gladys screamed. "You can't just
go around eating people!"

She was so mad,
that she stomped one foot,

then the other foot,
and then both feet at once.

Gladys lost her balance,
started to slip,

and fell into the pot.

"You crazy monsters!" Gladys hollered.
"Get me out of this stupid pot!"

Hilda and Rose tried and tried,

but they couldn't pull Gladys out of the pot.

"She's stuck," said Hilda.

"That's for sure," said Rose. "Stuck in a pot. Ha, ha, ha!"

Hilda and Rose laughed and laughed,
until suddenly...

the baby woke up and started to cry.

"Now look what you've done!" Gladys shrieked.
"You woke the baby up! I'm supposed to take care of her!
Stop laughing! I'm in charge!"
But Gladys couldn't do anything.

"I'll change the baby's diaper," said Hilda.
"And I'll get the baby's bottle," said Rose.
So Hilda and Rose took care of the baby,
and the baby stopped crying and smiled.

"I'm hungry," said Rose.
"So am I," said Hilda.

"I'm hungry and stuck," said Gladys.
"Stuck in a stupid pot."

That night, it was Hilda who warmed the spaghetti for their
dinner, while Rose took care of the baby.
And it was the best spaghetti they had ever tasted!